Between Friends

∞

ANGELA McCONNELL

Between Friends

∞

ANGELA MCCONNELL

ISBN: 978-1-941290-00-2

FIRST EDITION

Cover Art and Design by Jon McConnell
Interior design and illustrations by Angela McConnell

Seven Left Turns Publishing, Inc.
California, USA

This first one is for Les.

Table of Contents

§

"True friends stab you in the front."
OSCAR WILDE

I Take You

Erika touched the bite wound on her cheek and winced. It throbbed painfully, hot and sticky with blood.

A loud crash came from the hallway. She shrank back into the narrow space between the book-laden couch and a stack of crates, clutching a broken broomstick.

Tomorrow, she promised herself, she would call her granddaughter, leave him and this old house behind once and for all. This time she would do it.

It would mean breaking her promise. Her eyes filled with tears. He would feel so betrayed.

"Addie?" came a raspy whisper from the doorway.

She froze.

"Oh, Adeline, what happened to you, dear? Where did they take you? I miss you so."

Erika exhaled silently with a small measure of relief. He always mourned for Adeline at the end of these episodes.

"Adeline?" he called out from the doorway, his voice lifting up at the end like a lost child's. Erika felt an urge to go to him, but she knew he was just doing one of his tricks.

She covered her ears, held her breath, and focused on being invisible. It was the only bit of magic he had ever been able to teach her, and she wasn't very good at it. But maybe it would be enough to convince him she had just left and he'd move on down the hall looking for her—and hopefully lose himself in the rubbish-packed house until his senses returned to him.

Something fell with a clatter. She stifled a gasp. He was in the room.

He whined in the darkness, a chilling sound like a wounded animal. "Skin and Bones?" His voice changed to a low throaty growl. "Are you in there, dear?"

She broke out into a cold sweat ruining any chance of invisibility. He only called her that when he was being cruel. She gripped the broom handle tighter. Her arthritic joints complained with soft pops beneath her paper-thin skin.

"I heard that." He sounded delighted. "I know you're in there," he said with a laugh. "I can smell your worthless rotting corpse. What did you do with my sweet Adeline?" He whined again, raising the hair on the back of her neck. "Oh, poor Adeline."

A flashlight flicked on, a beacon in the clutter-filled living room.

"Skin and Bones, don't make me come get you," he warned.

She closed her eyes and started praying.

He gave an evil chuckle. "Very well. Ready or not, here I come!"

Erika listened in horror to the scrape of his nails as he scrambled over piles of old magazines and discarded electronics. His flashlight rose above the horizon of old newspapers and years-old junk mail like a tiny moon over a ruined cityscape. She sat stiff in the manner of prey, tracking his clumsy progress through the black, tangled room by his reckless flashlight and the two yellow coins of light that disappeared when he blinked.

Then the flashlight went dark and something large crashed to the floor. Her heartbeat thundered her ears, pounding like a doomsday drum. She held the broomstick out in front of her trembling.

Several minutes crept by, and she wondered if maybe he had knocked himself unconscious. She counted to 60 five times, then once more just to be sure. Still nothing.

It was safe.

She sighed in relief, which made her side ache. She probably had another broken rib.

A harsh light flicked on, and she cried out in fright. The ancient creature stood triumphant over her, holding the flashlight below his pointy chin. His eyes glittered, brown-gray and rheumy, a cataract frosting over one lens. Long, pointed ears rose up the sides of his head like prong horns, elderly cartilage curling up at the tips with hairs like iron wires.

His thin lips stretched across shark-like teeth, sepia shadows filling in the spaces between the yellowed ivory. His lower face was smeared with dark brown.

She realized it was blood...*her* blood.

"Hello, love," he said, his breath hot and sour. He licked his lips. "Shades of Goldemar, but don't you taste sweet? I think I would like seconds."

The creature snatched her by the shoulders and sank his teeth into her neck. He shook his head back and forth trying to rip her throat open, and she screamed as she felt herself cast into the darkness once again.

From This Day Forward

Erika had been to the edge of life before, this now familiar place of in-between. She was not afraid here, where her days of living passed by in streaks of light, good times and bad. They were too many to count, and they filled her within and without with a light that she recognized only as herself.

She watched her childhood blossom into adolescence, adolescence metamorphisize into adulthood, and adulthood atrophy into the most painful period of her life.

Then, like a gift, the memories slowed down and Erika cast eager eyes ahead as George's wake spun into view, the day her life truly began.

In Good Times

He arrived the night of George's wake, along with the strange storm clouds that hung low in the sky and cast the streets in an unearthly green light. Erika didn't notice him at the time, but he was there, a slippery shadow that moved between mourners, picking up empty plates and wiping up crumbs.

When her legs grew weak from the weight of the tears she refused to shed, he leaned against the back of her knees to brace her against the surge of black-attired folks who spun and eddied around her in their predictable circles. Around the buffet table they went, making awkward acquaintances in regrettable circumstances, gossiping about the recently dead behind the backs of hands.

These she heard, the whispered suppositions that she hadn't taken good enough care of poor George, that it was somehow her fault—and how depressing and cheap the lilies she had picked out for him looked.

Erika hated those people, George's "friends," with their white-teeth smiles and hooded vulture eyes. They didn't know anything about George, about what his last few years had been like. Her bitterness came not from the behind-the-back accusations though, but from the painful lump of guilt in her throat she knew she would never be able to swallow down.

Beneath the burning haze of such powerful dark emotions, no one saw the uninvited guest dip a spiteful finger into each one of the casserole pans, bringing a quick and thankful end to a joyless event.

Fifteen minutes later, urgently, and en masse, visitors made their goodbyes, their regrets sincere this time, before fleeing home to their bathrooms.

∞

It was raining when she returned alone to the house she had shared with George for the past 20 years, her car packed with unwanted casseroles and already-dying flowers. Her daughter offered to come along, help unload everything, but Erika wanted to spare her the embarrassment. Instead, she ended up pushing her daughter away, all the way back to Los Angeles.

She just wanted to be alone.

Erika parked in the drive, left everything in the car, and walked through the torrent without bothering to put up her umbrella.

A ragged hole gaped in the exterior wall of the living room where firefighters had cut away with their axes in order to remove George's body. Black plastic had been secured carelessly over the opening, and now flapped noisily in the wind, letting rain in with every gust.

She opened the front door and stared at the one clean spot in the living room, a vaguely George-sized space outlined with empty prescription bottles and trash.

This was all that was left.

She laid down in the spot where George died and closed her eyes, welcoming the rain that fell on her upturned face.

The state of their home was already cause for a great amount of unwanted attention and pity, but now she felt like a monster, changed into something undesirable by the mantle of widowhood and guilt. People at the wake couldn't get out of there fast enough, as if they were afraid close proximity to her might attract misfortune into their own lives.

Or maybe it was simply because it was cold and raining and they were eager to return home to their loved ones. She could understand that.

She thought of George's last words to her and cried. She couldn't believe he was gone.

∞

Erika awoke with a pillow slipped beneath her head and a blanket tucked carefully around her. She stared at the wall. The hole had been repaired—no, it looked as if the wall had never been damaged.

A framed picture of her and George from their trip to the Bahamas was hung precisely on the wall. She almost didn't recognize herself and George smiling at the camera, people she once knew. That was long before George had become bedridden and everything became painful.

She sat up slowly and looked around. The room had been cleaned up and organized, all evidence of chronic ill health and suffering cleared away. What magic had come to erase the last five years of hell?

∞

Erika discovered the stranger in the kitchen. It was only because she was looking for something extraordinary that she properly noticed him for the first time. Indeed, she had never seen anything quite like him.

He stood on a stool in order to reach the kitchen counter, trimming bright-faced daisies and arranging them into festive bunches in red plastic cups. He fluffed the blooms with odd, bulbous fingers tipped with sharp, black nails. His long pointed ears and hooked nose gave him an almost demonic appearance.

He caught her watching him and smiled, revealing a mouthful of sharp teeth, but she didn't feel afraid—she felt recognition. She saw the kindness in his eyes, the care with which he handled the flowers, and knew him to be a kindred soul who suffered, too, from a deep, unspeakable grief.

He dipped his head in a most gracious manner. "I hope you don't mind. It seemed you could use a little help, and it was getting pretty wet in here." His voice was soft, with the hint of a German accent.

Erika glanced back at the living room and flushed with embarrassment.

"They had difficulty getting him out," she said quietly.

He patted her gently on the arm and said the words she most needed to hear: "There is no shame in needing help from time to time. It is already in the past."

A sense of relief filled her to overflowing, and she looked away.

He politely pretended not to notice the tears Erika wiped away with her sleeve. Instead, he tickled a long-faced daisy with his fingertips until it giggled and beamed up at him, stretching its petals in joy.

"I don't make it a habit to intrude," he said, running his fingertips through the daisies to make them tinkle with laughter, "but I was passing by and saw you through the glass surrounded by all the ravens. I couldn't help myself. I'm a sucker that way."

"Ravens?"

"You know, all those two-faced co-workers and underlings, dumb old Cousin Edward who thinks there's a will with his name at every funeral, and those judgmental *bitches* from church—"

She laughed. "I like you."

He smiled shyly and offered her a daisy. "I like you too."

Erika took the daisy, and the little flower smiled up at her and waved cheerfully.

∞

His name was Chimmy, and he was a kobold, originally from Bavaria. Erika wasn't quite sure exactly what a kobold was, except she understood he wasn't human. He made that distinction quite clear.

Whatever he was, he was "in transition at the moment," so to speak, looking for work, a place to stay. His previous living situation had become untenable, he explained vaguely, some long complicated thing about a banishment, nothing he cared to revisit right now, if she didn't mind.

"My past," he said, with a great sense of regret, "is complicated in ways I find difficult to put to words."

She took his hands and said, "There is no shame in needing help from time to time. It's already in the past."

He smiled up at her with such open gratitude it made her heart ache. "You are too good."

"No, you are."

They grinned at each other in the manner of long-time friends, and she invited him to stay.

∞

Houses are hungry and needy beasts requiring constant, endless care and attention, and although her new handyman had unusual ways of doing things, there was no denying the results.

Chimmy only worked at night, while she slept, said it was easier for him to concentrate. And no matter what the project, it always took one night. After he built a new patio with a brick pizza oven, Erika begged to know his secret. Surely he used magic.

"What is this 'magic'?" he asked her, amused.

She gestured around the house. "This! What you do. How else could you accomplish these things overnight?"

He laughed at the notion. "My dear Erika, there is no magic. Everything I do myself. It is only a matter of how you see time and how I see time that you think it is an easy feat for me. Nay, there is no magic."

She ran her hands over the precisely-laid brick that lined the curved opening of the pizza oven. "Then how?"

He shrugged. "I am simply more—how do you say?— *efficient* than the average beast. Hell, I once helped an old man build a Japanese garden overnight, complete with a pond and a stone bridge. Of course, that was back when I had staff. Damn hard to find good help these days."

He loaded wood into the oven, then stuck two fingers in his mouth and gave a long, low whistle that sounded like a distant train. The wood erupted into flames, popping and crackling with sudden intense heat.

Erika gasped.

Chimmy turned and smiled his shark-tooth smile. "I'm hungry. Let's eat."

∞

Erika was unsurprised to learn Chimmy was also an excellent, if unconventional, fisherman.

They spent much of that first summer together drowsing on the shores of the lake, their fishing lines draped into the water, taking turns dipping into Chimmy's "Most Efficient Picnic Basket," which was always full of goodies no matter how much they filched from it.

It had been years since she had last gone fishing, long before George got sick, and she realized how much she missed it, the excuse to do nothing all day but nap in the shade and listen to the bugs zip across the water.

They spent countless afternoons out at the lake, whiling away the laziest hours. She even started to sketch again. Chimmy always brought a book, his long nose often touching the pages as he read behind the curtains of an old willow.

The best time was when dusk fell and the lavender shadows made it difficult to discern anything remarkable about the small, strange company she kept. That's when Chimmy got serious. "Going fishing" meant catching a fish, and he hated the idea of returning home empty-handed.

He would do this weird, sneaking creep that Erika found hilarious, all the way out to the end of the dock. Then he'd hang himself off the edge by his curly toes, his head beneath the surface, and sing to the fish.

Bubbles would rise up around him, popping into squishy-squashy notes of a upbeat little ditty that sounded a lot like "Happy Birthday," but not quite.

Fish are suckers for live music. Chimmy would give the courtesy of a little performance to the entranced fish that gathered around—it was only fair, after all—then without warning, let go of the dock and plunge jaws-first into his selected victim.

Erika enjoyed watching him—he was so silly!—but she still liked catching fish with a plain old pole. To each their own.

Afterwards, he'd spit on the hearthstones to ignite them red-hot, and they'd roast the fish under a starry sky.

It tasted divine.

And in Bad

Chimmy wasn't always fun and games. Sometimes he plunged into a deep blue sadness that faded him into the shadows of the house, silent and sulking, withdrawn. Erika learned early on to leave him alone when he got this way.

She had persisted once or twice in trying to draw him out, get him to talk to her, and he had lashed out at her with his claw-like nails. It was accidental. He never meant to hurt her. And anyway, it was superficial, never something that would require more than a few stitches, if she ever needed them.

Chimmy would instantly regret such incidents and apologize profusely, eagerly smoothing over wounds with soft fingers until the skin—and their friendship—was whole once more.

∞

Erika herself was not immune from episodes of crushing depression. She had her own demons. Sometimes, she would just see something that reminded her of George, and then she'd have to go lie down in her room for days.

Chimmy would leave trays of elaborate meals at her door in an attempt to lure her back into the light. Eventually, he'd win her over with something like a creamy custard...once with a simple pesto slathered on a slice of peasant bread.

He was an excellent baker.

∞

Inevitably, dark days were followed by periods of manic gaity, an insatiable eagerness to stuff themselves full of life and all it had to offer.

Together they filled the room where George died with souvenirs of good times: bowling trophies, sports equipment, several dozen kites—the detritus of a thousand pursuits of fun.

It was with some relief when Erika realized no more could be fit into the living room, and she closed the door for the last time.

But when she turned to face the rest of the house, her smile faltered. The hallway was constricted by stacks of banker boxes full of books and papers, so much so that she had to squeeze through sideways. The house had always been a mite bit cluttered, she could admit that much to herself, but she was going to clean it. Maybe next week she'd start.

She had to. Most of the rooms in the house were not far from being filled to the brim, and it gave her the sense she was running out of time.

∞

She shouldn't have made that awful promise the last time they played tennis together, but then, what choice did she have?

Ultimately, it was her own damn fault. She shouldn't have pushed him like she did. At 74 years old, Erika was more spry than she had ever been in her 40s, and frankly couldn't resist wiping up the court with her friend. She mercilessly walloped the ball towards opposite corners of the court, sending Chimmy running in a sweaty heap back and forth, back and forth, until he pitched his racket skyward in a rage.

It soared high above the trees, never to return.

He stood there for a moment on his side of the court, breathing heavily, his hair askew. She saw the look in his eye and turned to run. In an instant, he catapulted over the net and tackled her.

They fell to the ground, his fingers trembling around her neck, tensed to squeeze, eager to *squeeze*, and at the same time, fighting not to.

She hung on to his wrists and whispered, "It's okay, George. It's okay. I'm okay."

He let go then, a frightened look on his face. "I'm not George."

Afterwards, she threw up in the bushes, shaken and upset.

∞

Chimmy told her it was an inevitable affliction of the elderly of his kind. As kobolds aged beyond their normal lifespan— most respectable kobolds died before they got old, usually from accidents stemming from koboldy pursuits—their emotional memories start to unravel from deteriorating brains, causing repeated episodes of dementia and violence.

"How old are you?" she asked him.

"A lot older than you, I'm afraid," he said with a laugh. "Yes, I've certainly had more than my fair share of years."

"What can we do?"

He shrugged. "Usually, kin will watch closely over the elderly, and when it is time, when the bad outweighs the good, they do what needs to be done. But for kobolds in the wild, like me...."

Her mouth went dry with fear. "Are you going home?"

He shook his head. "I can't."

She was ashamed at how relieved she was to hear this. She knew he was desperately homesick, but she was also glad he couldn't go back. She reached for his hand, but he moved away, unable to meet her eyes.

"I was thinking maybe a fiery explosion or a fall from some great height. Something fun. I want to feel alive when I die," he said, trying to make light.

"What are you saying?"

He took her hands then and held them in his warm soft palms. He felt more real to her than anything in her life.

"I'm saying it's time for me to go, Erika. It's too dangerous for me to stay. I would never forgive myself if I—" He broke off, unable to put to words what they both feared.

Tears rushed down Erika's cheeks. "Where will you go?"

Chimmy smiled wistfully. "I was thinking the American Southwest. There's something very appealing to me about all that desolation. It would be a good place to go to die, a *safe* place."

She pictured Chimmy alone in the desert, taking his final breath beneath a wheel of stars with no one to mark his passing but a lone cactus. It wasn't right.

She also imagined spending the rest of her nights alone in the house that George built and knew her days would be numbered without her best friend.

"I can do it," she said. He looked up at her with hope in his eyes. She nodded. "Yes, yes, I can do it." She squeezed his hands. "Let me be your kin. It's not right for anyone to die alone, and I'd miss you horribly. I'll take care of you."

"But what if I hurt you again?" he asked.

"You won't," she said. "I'm your friend and your family. I will do what needs to be done. You can trust me."

The words slipped out before she could pull them back in, and she felt a twinge of unease. She shook her head, trying to clear it of doubts. Of course she could do what needed to be done when the time came. She had done it before.

Chimmy wrapped his hands around her neck again, this time gently, and she felt the familiar tingle of his healing touch lift the bruises from her neck and the fear from her heart.

His eyes were filled with tears. "I'm so sorry, Erika," he said. "Let this be the last time I lay injury upon you."

She touched her neck gingerly, the hurt gone. "I wish I could do for you what you do for me."

He shook his head. "It is a difficult thing you are offering," he said, pulling away. "It's not something to ask of friends, even if they are family. It is an unpleasant duty and a soul-heavy responsibility. Are you certain?"

"Of course." *Who else was there?*

He searched her face then smiled finally, his face full of gratitude. "How lucky I am to have you."

She hugged him close and whispered into his collar, "I love you too, Chimmy."

In Sickness

Her days sped by, witnessed one last time, a gift of death, and she moved closer and closer to the light, warm and compelling…and completely frightening.

Somewhere in the bright lights of Eternity the shades gathered, people who had gone before her, eager to welcome her into ghosthood. Her daughter was there, having died too young with too much distance between them. Erika felt her child reaching for her, desperate to finally close that distance, and Erika ached to go to her.

But George was also there, waiting, hungry to reclaim her, determined to punish her for what she did. His final words echoed in her head. She could still feel his grip on her collar and his hot poisoned breath in her face.

"I know what you did," he said over and over again, his voice full of hate, "and I will be waiting for you."

His shade loomed large, blocking the light of Eternity, eager to swallow her whole, and she fled like she did each time she came to this place. She wasn't ready. She was too afraid.

Maybe she would never be ready to face him…but she would never be sorry for what she did.

She swam against the soul tide that threatened to carry her to her inevitable fate, desperate for another way, and found it—a slender thread of hope—and pulled herself down from the heavens back to her earthly confines.

And in Health

She awoke cradled in Chimmy's arms. He was wiping at the bloody wound on her neck, sobbing. "Oh, Erika! I'm so sorry! Please be alive! Oh, God, please!"

She coughed, a deep, barking spasm that hurt her throat.

"Erika!"

"I'm okay," she whispered.

"Thank God!" He held her close, stroking her with his healing touch, desperate to make things right. He cried loudly, like a child, and she reached her arms around him.

"I'm okay," she said again. "It's okay. I'm fine."

He pulled away enough to see her face, then placed his hand on her bony chest as if to confirm for himself that her heart still carried on.

"Oh, child," he said, his face shiny with tears. He smoothed his thumb over the bite wound on her cheek, his soft touch erasing the wound and easing the sting. "This cannot go on."

Erika shook her head vigorously. "No! It's too soon! We still have time."

He held her firmly by the shoulders. "I tried to kill you. I *wanted* to kill you. It's not too soon, Erika. It's almost too late."

"But—"

"You made a promise." His face was determined…and desperate.

She looked away at a stack of books that teetered within the circle of fading flashlight, their dusty lines made wavery by her tears.

"It will be okay," he said.

She shook her head, angry. "No, it won't."

"Not at first," he admitted, taking her hand into his, "but it will be one day."

She allowed him to pull her to her feet.

"Let's go get you cleaned up. I'll put on some tea, and we'll speak of friendship."

And murder, she thought, following him into the darkness of the house.

∞

Mr. Purrbody, their swinging-tail cat clock, let out a melancholy meow to announce the arrival of midnight. Witching hour.

Chimmy tossed Mr. Purrbody a treat and gave him a little scritch beneath his chin. Mr. Purrbody purred loudly, filling the kitchen with good feelings.

Erika smiled at the cat clock. Mr. Purrbody had been Erika's cat, back when he was alive, the best cat she'd ever loved, and she couldn't bear to part with him. So Chimmy made him into a clock...and for the most part, Mr. Purrbody seemed content to spend eternity presiding over the kitchen wall.

Chimmy swept off the papers that covered the kitchen table with one hand and helped Erika into a chair.

"I'll make you some tea, my dear," he said, planting a kiss on her head.

At the touch of his lips, the headache that pounded against her skull receded, and she sighed in relief.

"Thank you, Chimmy," she said.

"It's the least I can do," he said. He looked miserable, like he wanted to say more. Instead, he turned and waded through the trash to the counter.

She watched her old friend make tea like he had a thousand times before. The counters had always been too tall for his small stature, but as the years and the debris accumulated— he washed and saved every food container that crossed their threshold—the floor slowly grew to meet the difference.

Chimmy wore his usual 1978 rummage sale find with the tag still stapled to the bottom hem, a shapeless avocado-green blouse stained with blood.

As he struggled to make enough room in the sink to fit a cup beneath the faucet, she noticed his gray hair hung in greasy strands over the back of his collar. His shoulders looked so thin and narrow. It wouldn't take much pressure to push a blade between them, into the back of his heart.

When did he become so old and pathetic?

Erika looked down at her own torn and blood-soaked house dress, at the bony knees that tent-poled the thin fabric. She smoothed the threadbare cloth across her skinny thighs with liver-spotted hands and grimaced.

She didn't know why she was so surprised Chimmy was getting old. She had already lived more years than was natural, thanks to Chimmy's talents. She wouldn't be surprised if she had bats in her belfry either.

All the people she once knew were gone now, even her poor daughter, disappeared into the frightening light of the Ever After. She ached for her daughter and suddenly wished she had allowed her to come home the night of George's wake. How different things might be!

Tears welled up. Back there in the dark, with Chimmy's teeth buried in her throat and blood running down both sides of her neck like hot water, she thought for certain that her luck had run out.

She plucked at her collar. The blood-stiffened fabric irritated her skin, and the coppery smell nauseated her, but she felt too exhausted to seek out something clean.

Chimmy turned around and held up two freshly washed coffee mugs in triumph. "See, Erika? Progress!" He smiled his shark-tooth smile. She wished he'd wash his face. The bottom half was brown with flecks of dried blood. "Now I've just got to find the damn tea bags."

He stumbled over old take-out containers piled along the counter and excavated an open drawer. The tips of his long pointed ears brushed the bottoms of the overhead cabinets, and he bumped his head on a cabinet door that hung open.

"Ow!" He rubbed his head. "Gotta get around to fixing that thing," he mumbled. It had been a long time since he had fixed anything, Erika realized.

As he dug around, he sang, "Damn tea bags, damn tea bags, where are you, you *goddamn* tea bags?"

Erika smiled in spite of everything. There was the old Chimmy again.

"How do you feel about pomegranate-orange tea?" Chimmy asked from halfway inside the cabinet.

"I feel pretty good about it." Erika chuckled.

Chimmy looked so waifish in that ugly old blouse. She told him so.

He rolled his giant bloodshot eyes with a toss of of his head and tore off the tops of the two tea packets, popping them neatly into the mugs. "You've always been jealous of me," he said, with a sniff.

She laughed. It was always Chimmy's sense of humor that saved her. She missed the old days.

"I wish we could go fishing," she said suddenly, thinking of those early days, lazy and sun-drenched.

"I could handle a big fried fish right about now," he agreed, setting the teapot on the stove.

How had it been 50 years already? Life felt so short.

"Hey, remember that time we brought home all those sunfish, and the cat got into them?"

Chimmy laughed, a deep belly laugh that rose up into a cackle. "How could I forget? He ate three of them and hid the rest in my room, which I found—"

"Three days later," they both said together, then laughed again.

Chimmy shook his fist at Mr. Purrbody in mock anger. The kitty clock yowled at the memory.

That fish was so tasty! Kitty has no regrets, not a single one!

Mr. Purrbody's pendulum tail curled and uncurled, wanting for a moment to jump down from the wall and stir up trouble like old times.

The teapot squealed energetically, eager to be included in the merriment. Chimmy lifted it off the burner and poured its piping hot contents into mugs. He set them down on the kitchen table.

"Thank you," Erika said, cupping her hands around the warm ceramic. The tea smelled delightful.

"Did you want sugar?" he asked, looking around a bit hopelessly at the mess.

"No, don't worry about it, dear," she said, even though she hated tea without it. It'd probably take him an hour to find it anyway—

"Actually, I could do with a spot of sugar, if you don't mind." Anything to delay the inevitable turn of conversation.

"Of course," he said, and got back up with a groan. "I could have sworn I saw some in one of the drawers."

He shuffled back over to the kitchen counter and started pulling open the drawers again, humming an old gameshow tune. It reminded her of the time when—

"Hey," she said, "you remember the time we got that karaoke machine and the neighbors called the cops on us because they thought we were torturing an animal?"

Chimmy snorted. "I'll never forget that cop's face when I told him my mommy wasn't home." He sniggered as he made his way through the cabinets. "That poor confused man—aha! Always behind the third door!" He held up a bowl of sugar in triumph and hobbled back to the table.

He plunked down the sugar and fell into his chair with a great sigh. He took a noisy sip of his tea, then eyed Erika.

"I remember when you decided we were going to learn cake decorating and go into business for ourselves."

Erika rolled her eyes at him as she reached for the sugar. "*I* decided? I distinctly remember you saying, 'Let's make gum paste roses. It'll be *easy*!'" She tipped some sugar into her cup. "Spoon?"

"Oh, sorry." Chimmy creaked back to his feet to fetch one. "That red velvet cake was a disaster, wasn't it?"

She cringed at the memory. "All I know is when I looked in the toilet the next day, I thought I was dying."

Chimmy threw his head back and cackled. "I remember the sounds that were coming from the bathroom. I thought you were dying too!"

They both laughed. Laughing at Death. It felt good, she thought. She was glad he was finally over his episode.

"My goodness, we've done everything, haven't we?"

Chimmy dropped back into his chair and handed her the spoon. "I think so." He ticked off items with bony fingers. "There was scuba diving, kite flying, puzzles—"

"Ceramics, paper-making, frisbee golf," she added.

"Roller derby, croquet—don't we still have that set?"

"We have three."

"Oh, yeah. I suppose we quit a few times."

"Yes. Vicious game, croquet." Erika shaking her head at the memory. "Worse than Monopoly."

"Yeah, brings out the worst in people." He started to chuckle, then hung his head low, his long nose dropping almost into his cup. "I am sorry about your face and—" He patted his neck, too ashamed to finish.

She reached out and patted his hand. She wanted to tell him it was fine, she was fine, but she didn't have the energy to lie anymore.

"We've had a good time together, haven't we?" Chimmy asked her. He looked almost pleading.

She smiled. "I don't know about you, dear friend, but I've had the time of my life." Her eyes filled with tears.

"Have I been good to you?"

"For the most part," she said, trying to make light.

He looked stricken, and she squeezed his fingers gently. "You've been so very good to me. You saved me. If you hadn't come after George died, I don't know what would have become of me."

Chimmy blushed. "You are a wonderful lady, Erika. You would have done just fine without me."

"Maybe fine," she conceded, "but not extraordinary. You have made my life *magical.*"

He smiled gratefully and rubbed his oddly smooth finger-tips over the tops of her hands, gently erasing the persistent ache from her joints and the liver spots from her skin. They returned quickly these days, and Chimmy's touch was a relief.

"I don't think we have much time left," he said as he worked. He kept his gaze down.

Erika hoped he had forgotten. She hoped they wouldn't have to talk about this. She meant to argue with him, but instead, she whispered, "I know."

"I hear voices. They whisper to me behind every corner."

"What do they say?" she asked, afraid to know.

His voice shook. "They say terrible things. They want me to *do* such terrible things. To you." He looked up at her then. Tears streaked down his face. "I'm scared, Erika. You've got to end this."

"Oh, Chimmy...." Erika looked around the crowded, rubbish-filled kitchen and thought about all the good times they had together. Mr. Purrbody purred softly from his perch on the wall.

How can this all come to an end? she thought.

"You'll be okay," he said gently.

She stared at her tea. They both knew his death meant her own death. Surely, without his magic, nature would take its course as it was hungry to do. But she told him the lie he needed to hear.

"I'll be fine. Maybe I'll go live with Kristen. She asks every time she calls. I'll go play great-great-grandma, be with my own kind."

Chimmy laughed at that.

"I do love my family, you know."

"I know."

"But *you're* my family."

"I know."

They sat there at the kitchen table, poking their tea bags with their spoons. Erika wished everything would stop right that moment, their last time together spent reminiscing over orange-pomogranate tea.

But Chimmy got up and pulled open a drawer. He drew out a large carving knife and ran it across a broken whetstone several times.

Erika watched as he scraped away silver hairs from his arm with the blade. Satisfied, he returned to the table and presented the knife to her.

"I don't know what to do," she said.

"A quick stab," he said, pointing to the center of his narrow chest, "straight in the heart."

She felt sick. "What if I can't do it? What if you suffer?"

His face hardened. "You must. Better I suffer now, for a brief time, than suffer for the rest of my unnatural life for some unforgivable sin later." His voice broke. "Please take it."

She knew he suffered from the burden of mistakes he made in the past, but the thought of putting that knife in him—

"What if I don't agree? I think it's too soon. What if I refuse?"

Her voice trailed off. She was exhausted. She had long ago lost count of how many times they had had this conversation. How much longer could she keep helping him through these episodes with the drugs? If he ever found out—

"You made a promise," he said, breaking into her thoughts. "Please take it."

She looked down. She did make a promise. And she had always honored her promises.

He waited patiently for her to come to the conclusion he knew she must come to. She closed her eyes, and for a brief second, allowed herself to imagine what it was like for him, a stranger in a strange land, going crazy, descending into darkness.

Chimmy was her best friend, and he was asking her for help.

Erika picked up the knife and laid it next to her mug.

"We're like 'War of the Roses,' aren't we?" she said with a sad laugh.

He snorted. "You don't look anything like Kathleen Turner, dearie."

"Hah! Well, you're no young Michael Douglas yourself."

They laughed. Erika realized this was the last time they would ever laugh together. She reached over and took both his hands into hers. "Thank you, Chimmy."

"For what?"

"For being my friend. For saving me."

He held her face, tears tracing down his deep laugh lines. "You saved me too, you know. I found you when I needed someone the most, and you didn't turn me away."

"Never," she said. "I know a good soul when I see one."

Chimmy cast his eyes down and drew away. Erika thought she had caused him insult somehow and reached for his hand again, but he slapped her away with a snarl.

For an instant, their eyes met. The madness had returned.

He started to move towards her. She snatched the knife up from the table and whipped it around as hard as she could. A thin red line appeared across his knobby throat.

He looked stunned for a second, then drew a finger across the wound. He looked at the blood, then at her.

"You're going to have to cut much deeper than that, Skin and Bones," he hissed.

She cried out in fear, and Chimmy's face softened for a second. Erika watched transfixed as he struggled to hold on to his sanity. He gripped the edges of the table with pale knuckles and gave her one last desperate look.

"Please. Just do it," he begged her.

She sat frozen in her chair, the knife held out in front of her like a cross, its blade pointed heavenward. Its fine edge shimmered red.

He climbed over the table towards her, his face sharpening cruelly as the madness took over. His nose pressed against hers, and his chest pinned the knife between them. He breathed in deeply as if he could taste her, then exhaled, stirring her hair with his ancient, rotting air.

"I remember how you taste, sweet and murky, like spiced wine and old soul, salty like ocean tears," he whispered. "Your youth and innocence was the most intoxicating honey elixir on my privileged, undeserved tongue. God save me, I wanted to drink deeply of your eternal soul and steal you within me forever. I'm so, so sorry, my sweet Adeline."

He opened his eyes and screamed. "You!"

Erika braced herself, but then Chimmy's eyes softened in recognition. "Erika?"

She held his gaze, steeling herself to be brave, to be strong enough for him.

"I am your friend Erika," she said, staring into his frightened eyes, "and I love you, Chimmy. You are a *good* person."

Chimmy's face twisted with warring emotions. His mouth worked as he tried to tell her something.

"What? What is it?"

He forced the word out through clenched teeth. "Run."

"But Chimmy—"

"*RUN!*" he screamed in her face, his breath hot and furious.

She bolted back in her chair, but he caught her by her arms, digging his nails deep into her flesh. Red bloomed on her sleeves like rose petals.

He scraped his dry, hot tongue across her cheek, rasping her flesh on fire. She screamed in pain.

He dug his nails in deeper and shook her until her teeth rattled.

"You will tell me what you did with my sweet Adeline, or I will cut off all of your limbs and boil you into a stew and eat every last miserable piece of gristle."

She sobbed. Chimmy was lost.

With a cry, she lunged to her feet and drove the kitchen knife straight up into the ancient kobold's bottom jaw. Hot blood spilled from his mouth and over her hands.

She screamed and ran.

His gurgled howls echoed after her as she crashed down the hallway, stumbling over stacked laundry baskets filled with art supplies, old celluloids, antique glass, boxes—everywhere there was paper and boxes, corners and jagged edges.

His agonized cries filled the remaining spaces of the house, making it difficult to think.

She staggered towards the laundry room. If she could just get outside—

The back door was blocked with a waist-high drift of empty water bottles. Erika plunged through and struggled with the doorknob, her hands slippery with blood. Finally, the door gave with a sticky pop, and she pulled it open a little ways against the recycling.

"I will cook one limb at a time," a murderous voice raged somewhere behind her, "so that I might enjoy your company for several dinners. I do love leftovers!"

He was coming!

She scooped frantically at the plastic bottles, trying to make enough room to open the door enough. Winter air stole in with the brightness of the full moon, limning the room in blue.

A screech rose up behind her. Claws ripped down the back of her housedress, splitting her skin open. Erika screamed and twisted to face the murderous creature. Hundreds of empty plastic bottles surged around them as they flailed at each other. Somehow she got her feet up against his chest and kicked with all her might.

As she struggled to her feet, something wet and stinging splashed into her face. Lighter fluid.

She wiped at her eyes, the fumes stinging. He stood over her holding up the can of lighter fluid, an unlit cigarette poking out of his thin lips.

"I've got *such* a craving for barbecue," he said, flicking a lighter to the end of his cigarette and setting it aglow.

Erika spun and hauled on the doorknob. More lighter fluid splashed against her back, setting her open wounds ablaze. She jammed herself into the narrow opening, one foot on the back porch.

The kobold blew smoke at her as he watched her struggle to get out. He smiled wickedly. "Roasted skin and bones," he said. "I like it when the skin gets crunchy. Mm-*mm!*"

He flicked the cigarette at her. It bounced off her arm and landed in the pile of trash between them. Flames ignited angry red lines of lighter fluid, filling the small room with black smoke. Panicked, Erika shoved herself the rest of the way through into the freezing air outside.

Then she heard Chimmy cry out. "Erika! Erika! What's happening?" He sounded so scared.

She paused for a moment, then pushed her head back inside. It *was* Chimmy. He stood behind a rising wall of fire, his eyes wide with panic.

"What do I do?" he cried.

"Chimmy!" she yelled. "Come on! Get out of there! Just jump through! Now!"

She waved at him to hurry.

He shook his head, the flames rising between them. "I have to find Adeline!"

"No, Chimmy, there's no time! You have to get out now!"

"I have to find her! I can't leave her!"

"Chimmy—"

"I can't leave her!"

"Adeline is *dead!*" Erika screamed.

Chimmy stared at her, stunned.

"She's dead, Chimmy."

"No! How can you know that?"

Tears ran down Erika's face. She couldn't put to words what she knew in her heart was true. It would kill him.

Chimmy backed away. "You're *wrong!* I have to find her!" He turned and disappeared back into the house.

The heat and smoke drove her back out onto the porch. She gently pulled the door shut and watched the orange flames flicker on the other side of the glass.

In Joy and in Sorrow

Chimmy did eventually get to see the American Southwest, but only to visit. They hauled a vintage Airstream behind Erika's old Cadillac and smoked Virginia Slims just because it made them feel cool.

It was so much fun. Erika never felt so carefree. They ate Pie à la Mode at roadside diners and sang enthusiastically along to staticky radio stations that cut in and out across the baking desert.

But in the evenings around the campfire, Chimmy grew pensive and close-mouthed. Erika would awaken in the middle of the night to the soft snick of the Airstream's door closing behind him, and then again, when he would return, at the first light of dawn, slipping back into his bunk like a lover on the stray.

One night as they sat in front of the dwindling campfire watching the stars trace their infinite circles of light, she screwed up the courage to ask him where he was sneaking off to.

Chimmy didn't answer for a long time, and she wondered if he would. Finally, he let out a long sigh.

"I suppose it was foolish of me to think I could hide it from you," he said, poking at the coals with a stick. He looked at her with tear-filled eyes. "I have been searching for someone, someone I lost."

She sat very still and said nothing, afraid if she spoke, he'd swallow his secret back down forever.

His voice rose barely above a whisper, his secret so heavy. "It is the reason I was set to roam the world. My benefactor placed in my care his young daughter Adeline. Oh, Erika! I wish you could have met her. What a sweet-souled little child, all heart and warmth. You would have loved her too." He shook his head, wiping his eyes with his sleeve. "She showed me what the world really looked like, and it's so goddamn beautiful."

He raised his arms to prove his point, embracing the star-encrusted sky above the stately saguaros that held vigil around their intimate campsite.

"I was taking her to her mother in Stuttgart. The train station in Munich was busy that day, and I—I got confused. I looked away for one moment—I needed directions—and she—" His voice caught, and he looked at Erika with pleading eyes. "She *disappeared*."

"Oh, Chimmy—"

"She was just gone! And no one would help me. I looked everywhere for that little girl. *Everywhere.* I turned the entire city upside down. And when I think what someone might have done with her—oh, *God!*"

He clutched his stomach. "Of course they blamed me. What else could they think? But I swear, I would never, ever hurt that child. Never." He shook his head emphatically. "I looked away for one moment, Erika," he whispered.

"I believe you, Chimmy," she said softly.

"I cared for her from the day she was born, and I loved her as my own. I've spent a lifetime looking for Adeline, hoping to recognize her eyes in the face of a woman grown, praying that somehow she still got to live out her natural life, unaware of her true identity. I just cannot consider the alternative."

Chimmy's words hung like smoke over the fire, low and frightening. He leaned forward and stared into the flames. After a moment, he spoke again.

"I have this nightmare, though, that comes often, and sometimes I wonder if my memory of what happened isn't quite right, if maybe I did something...*bad.*"

He looked horrified and confused. "I can't remember! How could a little girl just disappear?"

Erika moved to sit next to him and hugged his arm. "I will help you look for her," she told him. "Whatever you need."

"It is enough that you call me friend."

"I call you family," she reminded him. "Thick or thin, 'til death do us part."

He smiled sadly. "I love you, Erika."

She nodded, unable to answer back right away. "I love you too, Chimmy."

He leaned his head against her shoulder and sighed.

"Are you afraid of dying?" she asked suddenly.

Chimmy shook his head, his eyes fastened on the stars. "No, I yearn for it. It's the one place I haven't looked for her."

Tears spilled down Erika's cheeks.

"Are you afraid?" he asked her gently.

She held his arm tighter and nodded, unable to answer.

He stroked her hair and forehead, catching up her worries and fears with his strange fingers and flicking them into the fire where they exploded in tiny ruby sparks.

"Don't be afraid. My people believe Death is simply another place, and that all who went before will be waiting for us."

Erika thought about George and shivered. That's what she was most afraid of.

'Til Death Do Us Part

"Can you tell me again how the fire started?"

Erika shrugged, weary to explain it again. "It was an accident. I was going through our lighter collection, refilling the empty ones. I went to test one of them, and everything just caught."

"Well, thank Goldemar, you're okay," Chimmy said, his face full of concern. "You need to be more careful. You could have really gotten hurt. It's a miracle the garden hose wasn't frozen in this weather."

Erika nodded. "I know. I know."

She tucked the soot-streaked blanket around Chimmy's narrow shoulders and checked the thick bandage beneath his chin. Then she reached for the hot water bottle and laid it in Chimmy's lap. He gathered it up gratefully, cradling it like an infant. His eyes were wet.

"What a time for me to have one of my fainting spells."

He shook his head.

"What is it?" she asked.

"I feel like I've forgotten something important," he said, "something I shall never find again." He looked up at her beseechingly, struggling against the murkiness the drugs brought on. "Have I been good to you, my friend?"

She touched his grizzled cheek. "Always."

"You would tell me otherwise, wouldn't you?"

"Of course I would."

"You promise?"

He was so earnest, so desperate to believe. It was hard to say how long the drugs would last before the shine would creep back into his eyes and he would become...difficult again.

"I promise," she said, giving his hand a squeeze.

He smiled at her, his anxiety put to ease.

It wasn't a lie, Erika told herself. Even now, for her, the good outweighed the bad. She only wanted a little more time, another day, another hour.

She patted her housecoat pocket to assure herself the tube of blue powder was still there. She knew steel was the kobold standard, but she was never going to be able to do it properly. She looked guiltily at the wad of gauze bunched under his chin and remembered how he had screamed.

At least this way, they could share one last cup of tea together, then find peace wherever it was they were meant to go.

Or at least Chimmy could. She knew he was desperate to see Adeline again, to find forgiveness for the unforgivable.

But there was no forgiveness waiting for Erika on the other side, just George. And she knew he would never forgive her for what she did. He meant to make her pay, and he would wait forever if he had to.

So what was one more lie if it meant one more day?

Ray Bradbury Lives!

I was 15 years old the first time I went to hear Ray Bradbury speak. I rode with a friend and her mom out to a cramped little library in the middle of the desert, to a tiny town called Lucerne Valley. It was so old-school you could still see where they used to park the covered wagons.

And it was packed.

We had to park way out among the Joshua trees and walk like concertgoers through rows of cars up to the brightly-lit library. We wormed our way through excited book nerds and squeezed in, ducking beneath a latticework of elbows until we reached an open spot on the floor near the front, where we sat cross-legged like good little children.

I couldn't believe it. There he was! In the flesh! Mr. Ray Bradbury, Celebrated Storyteller and National Treasure—the guy who wrote *Fahrenheit 451*!—with his gleaming white hair, thick black glasses, and the biggest smile I've ever seen on a human.

He was seated in a chair, his arms held open to gather us in, and we leaned forward hungrily like sunflowers lean toward the dawn. And like the dawn, he inspired, pink and breathless, and he told us about the things he loved best.

Mr. Bradbury loved carnivals and Buck Rogers, dinosaurs and films, monsters and mysteries. He painted his life for us in big splashes of white on blue, electric on mystical, and we all fell in love with him.

It was a grand tour through his joyful childhood, a neighborhood of miracles and lightning men, and through the looking glass to his adulthood and legendary career, a serendipitous landscape shaped by the pursuit and celebration of those things he loved so much.

After storytelling time, I waited in the autograph line with my copy of *The Toynbee Convector*. Mr. Bradbury inscribed it to **Ages!**, a name I was trying out at the time because I was 15 and nerdy and writing epic fantasy. I was beyond stoked.

If there could be only one word used to describe Ray Bradbury, it would have to be joy. It burned bright and constant, and was unavoidably catching.

I left that little tic tac of a building burning with the afterglow of a religious experience. As we moved into the line of headlights that traced the way back across the dark-blue desert towards home, my young writer's heart burst with possibility and ached for the future.

The second time I got to see Ray Bradbury speak was maybe a year later. He was a keynote speaker at a writer's convention at the local university. I hitched a ride with Mr. Brown, my English teacher, who was way cool. He drove with one foot on the dash like a teenager and treated me like a fellow writer. I felt very grown-up.

This time, instead of a brightly lit library full of excited chattering people, Mr. Bradbury spoke in a hushed and darkened theater, his white hair set aglow by stage lights, and we got to see him for what he really was.

Just like before, he returned us to his childhood, straight to the traveling carnival where his 12-year-old self met Mr. Electrico, who sizzled on his electric chair, and knighted and delighted a young Ray Bradbury with a sword full of lightning and commanded him: "Live forever!"

Down in the trenches of the theater, his words ran up and down everyone's chair legs, connecting us all like a lit fuse, and I realized suddenly it was Ray Bradbury who was Mr. Electrico, knighting and igniting *us*, telling *us* to go, live forever!

Kapow!

I left the theater, electricity still humming through my veins, my brain and heart on fire. What a magician! To be able to incite such emotion through words! Provoke tears of hope, declarations of love, and to make people want to jump to their feet and hurry—*hurry*—rush out into the world and fall head over heels in love.

I knew that's what I wanted to do! Not just write stories that entertained, but stories that connected, heart to heart, soul to soul. I wanted to turn on some lights and shout from the rooftops and make people cheer! And then do it all over again!

They were selling tape-recordings afterwards. I swallowed my embarrassment and borrowed five dollars from my teacher to purchase a copy. It was worth it.

At the very beginning of the recording, you can hear the space of the auditorium, the sounds of breaths being held and released, feet shuffling, laughter and murmurs. I am somewhere on that tape, my 16-year-old self, an indiscernible part of that vague mix of noise and audience, about to be set on fire and launched into the future.

Two decades later, I'm still falling in love, still writing stories and yelling from rooftops, still trying to find my way to Forever.

And I still have that five-dollar tape, a little piece of Ray Bradbury's ghost now, his voice hailing alive and joyful from the Great Beyond.

It shows up now and again, when spirits get low and closets get cleaned out, a relic from a past life, a reminder of what is possible. It's a spiritual fortifier for me, extra mana, a can of Popeye's spinach.

Each time I listen to the tape, I discover a deeper truth that I wasn't long-lived enough to understand before, and I wonder what mysteries my future self will uncover the next time I revisit it.

In this way, Mr. Bradbury has become an old friend, a mentor, a hero, charging me up and setting me off. And every time he commands me from across the void, all the way from 1990, *"Live forever!"*, I am sent careening back to my keyboard, 16 years old again, the future electric and brilliant with the impossible once more.

Dear Reader...

Holy smokes! Fire up the torpedoes! It's time to launch this baby!

First of all, thank you so much for reading! I really appreciate it. I believe a story is never finished until it has been shared with another. And now that you have read my little tale, we are something of friends now, I hope. We've traveled places together. We know the same people. Shoot, that makes us downright accomplices, which makes it even more fun!

So if we're going to get into all kinds of trouble together, I should introduce myself. My name is Angela McConnell, and I write speculative fiction, which is a fancy way of saying weird tales, science fiction cozies, suburban fantasy, creature features, magic realism, occasional horror, and supernatural chick lit (you'll see).

Between Friends is my first title through my wee baby company Seven Left Turns Publishing, Inc. It's been a long time and a lot of work getting here, and I can't tell you how excited I am to finally be able to share with you what I've been working on.

I had a lot of help making *Between Friends* into a reality, and I have to give a great big thanks and shout-out to my brother Jon McConnell, the artist who created and designed the cover. Jon took a basic, straightforward concept and turned it into a living, breathing moment from the story that exceeded all my expectations. It turned out beautifully. (So glad I campaigned for a baby brother!)

Gotta give a shout-out to Pam Peacock, a.k.a. The Snarky Peacock, my intrepid, awesomely geeky, and surprisingly Vulcan-like graphic designer, who distilled the spirit and intent of Seven Left Turns Publishing, Inc., into an awesome logo reminiscent of Route 66 and classic 1950s. Love it!

Grateful thanks go to my best friend Kellie Flores for always believing in me and for giving me that final nudge I needed to do interior illustrations.

"People like 'em," she said. "I find them charming."

I hope so. I had a lot of fun drawing them, and I hope that what I lack in experience, I was able to make up for in charming. :)

Lots and lots of love to Ray Bradbury, who set generations of imaginations on fire, and who was warm and welcoming to this geeky little kid.

For the author photo, I thought about putting forward a nice, respectable, totally flattering portrait from behind which I could conduct the trickeries of my trade for years to come, Doris-Gray style…but that didn't sound like any fun.

So I called on Andrew Bramasco, a very funny and *way* talented photographer who hails from the Great County of Orange, California. I met up with Andrew at a glass artist's studio in Downtown L.A. (*Thanks, Mike!*), with my five-year-old little girl in tow. We brought with us props, costumes, wigs, and a big bag of junk food and beer, our sole focus and intent to have a super silly time and get it on film.

Mission accomplished.

My beautiful sister-in-law Amanda McConnell, an insanely talented costume designer, and Cassie Landis-Cushard, one of the classiest ladies I know (who can rock a mustache better than any man!), helped style the shoot. There was foam-sculpting, a potato launcher, lots of duct tape, and tons of embarrassing pictures…the above photo being only the first of many.

(You'll have to stay tuned if you want to see the rest of them, including the one of me wearing a sock and hiding in bushes that are **not** marijuana plants, *Dad!*)

The beehive may be a little over the top, but I've made it my mission to entertain, and sometimes a gal just needs a really big hairdo to do that.

That and more fun stories.

So next month, I'll be releasing *Nympho*, a story about a young woman who wakes up to discover she is growing horns. (I *hate* it when that happens!)

The following month I'll bring you *Animal Control*, in which a raging wildfire casts a frightening pall over a foothill community, and a young father-to-be tries to catch whatever it is that's eating the neighborhood cats.

And I can hardly wait until later this summer, when I get to introduce you guys to my new science fiction series called *Pacifica:*

> "Liz Robinson never expected life as a water farmer on a newly colonized planet to be easy, but add in a three-year-old with erupting molars, a missing husband, storms that last for months, and man-eating monsters, and frankly, life's a bitch. And she's about to punch that bitch in the face."

If you'd like to be notified when new stories come out, feel free to sign up for my newsletter at www.angelamcconnell.com.

I also blog daily there, share adventures, talk story, and implicate my friends through thinly-veiled nicknames. Come on by and say hi. :)

Again, many thanks for reading, and as always, may the Schwartz be with you.

Shout-Outs!

Sometimes it really does take a village to raise one of these little guys, and I am so fortunate to have such an awesome bunch of Village People in my life.

A bouquet of begonias to Murphy, for reading everything I've ever given him, and for discovering the way.

Smooches and hugs to my fellow writers, the Third Ninjas Omniscient, who are awesome to me in ways I can't even say… because we're ninjas, you know, and ninjas aren't supposed to cry. So…Ninja Dahazee, Ninja Jeff, Ninja Sonja, and Ninja Laura…*domo arigato* and *kumpai!*

Much gratitude goes to my fellow Failure Club members Kellie Flores, Amanda McConnell, Mona Madry-Adams, Jefferson Adams, Kathy Jaffe, and Marian Iskandar, who have cheered me on, called my bluffs, kicked me in the beheinie, and supported me in ways I could never quantify. Thanks, guys! You're the best!

Finally, and most importantly, I have to thank my Mom and Dad, for which none of what I do would be possible, and Lester and Leia, without whom none of it would be worthwhile. I love you.

For more entertainment, please visit

WWW.ANGELAMCCONNELL.COM